Finally Loving Forward

A Collection of Essays on Learning to Love Again

Samantha Gail B. Lucas

Ukiyoto Publishing

All global publishing rights are held by

Ukiyoto Publishing

Published in 2023

Content Copyright © Samantha Gail B. Lucas

ISBN 9789360165864

All rights reserved.
No part of this publication may be reproduced, transmitted, or stored in a retrieval system, in any form by any means, electronic, mechanical, photocopying, recording or otherwise, without the prior permission of the publisher.

The moral rights of the author have been asserted.

This book is sold subject to the condition that it shall not by way of trade or otherwise, be lent, resold, hired out or otherwise circulated, without the publisher's prior consent, in any form of binding or cover other than that in which it is published.

www.ukiyoto.com

Acknowledgments

I would like to thank my mother, Cheryl, and my late father, Mario, for investing in my education and encouraging me to follow my dreams.

I would also like to thank my partner Miguel Lopez for always rooting for me.

I would also like to thank everyone who supported me and my books. Thank you for also buying a copy of this book! I hope your kindness will be returned to you tenfold.

Contents

Introduction	1
I Learned to Love Myself	4
I Moved On From Rejection	7
I Developed My Skills	10
I Built My Confidence	13
I Learned to Thrive Alone	16
I Dated to Marry	19
I Dated Intentionally	22
I Learned to Say No	25
I Journaled About Love	28
I Became Happy No Matter What	31
I Became Supportive of My Partner	34
I Left Toxic Relationships	37
I Became the Partner that I Wanted to Have	40
I Built a Life with My Partner	43
I Focused on My Relationship	46
About the Author	*48*

Introduction

I learned how to love again when I went through a particularly nasty breakup. I lost the friends that I shared with my ex, because I chose to begin again without his circle. I chose to leave behind the places that we shared, and the playlists that reminded us of our memories together. I donated all the clothes from that era. I had nothing to remind me of him, except for the journal entries that I wrote about him. With nothing else left but myself, I decided to focus on myself by loving myself.

I took care of myself. I needed to regain my energy, so I ate healthy food and worked out. I read books again because being in that relationship prevented me from enjoying the books that I loved. I had more time for myself again, so I built new playlists, wrote new journal entries, and watched movies which I did not see with him. I learned to laugh again. I crocheted, brewed coffee, and bought new clothes. Before I knew it, I was moving forward.

I met my current partner after I focused solely on myself. By making self-love as my number one priority, I actually became attractive again. I was able to start a new relationship because I was ready to share the love that I felt for myself. And because I was secure in my own journey, I was able to have a new life with a partner who finally appreciated the real me. It was refreshing to simply be myself and not put any effort into being cool. He loves me because I am already cool enough for him. And I think that acceptance is the whole point of loving forward.

When we love forward, we accept ourselves. When we learn to accept the idea of ourselves with the person who makes us happy, then that is when we finally love another person in a forward direction. We are no longer stagnant, because this love finally has direction. It is leading us to the right path, and it is essential that we both know that this is how home really feels like.

For me, home is not a place. It is a feeling. I feel at home with the person who accepts me wholeheartedly, and that is myself. I feel at home with my partner, because he is also a complete person, and he accepts me for who I really am. I feel that loving forward is a direction more than a destination, and I would like to share my journey by writing this book.

It is my hope that more people will see the wisdom in loving with direction and purpose. It is my dream that more people will accept themselves for who they really are. And it is my prayer that more people will find the love that makes them feel at home.

So let me share my story so that you too can *finally love forward!*

I Learned to Love Myself

I realized how much self-love has taken a backseat in my life when I became single again after a string of unsuccessful relationships. They were unhealthy partnerships because these men really made it a point to verbalize their displeasure over my unique traits. From my writing career, which I started from scratch, to my easy, forever summer fashion sense, it was always a case of me lacking in some department of life. Looking back, I think they were just jealous because I have my writing career, my fashion style which is not dictated by labels or brands, and a life that is filled with joy and fulfillment. However, since I was with dissatisfied partners these past few years, I still adjusted to their whims and weird sense of entitlement. It was unhealthy, so I really felt free and relieved when I finally became single again. It was during this time that I was able to regroup and focus on myself again.

I learned to love myself once more.

I started with journaling. I listed down the things that I was grateful for. I remember writing how thankful I was that I did not marry this guy, and that

I am not obliged to agree whenever he brings me down. I was grateful for my workout routine, which I have always done for my own health and well-being, and not to please some guy. I was thankful for my writing career, because I know that my story can help other people and inspire those going through similar struggles. I was thankful for my breakup, because I knew that it was not a healthy relationship to begin with. And I was grateful for myself, because I was strong enough to handle life and all its surprises.

I worked on myself by reminding myself that self-love is only the beginning. It is the actionable steps that I will take to make this love matter. So, I wrote books on the lessons I have learned from my failed relationships, and my own relationship with myself. I bought new clothes to replace the ones that I already donated because they reminded me of the wrong people. I made sure that I always looked neat and presentable, even when I was simply lounging around at home. And I fed my mind by reading books and listening to podcasts. It was important to me that my mindset was centered on growth and self-improvement, and I reminded myself that learning is a lifelong journey.

I am constantly working on myself, and self-love is a major component of that process. I keep tabs on myself, and I make sure to correct myself whenever

I am wrong. I know that I need feedback, so I often ask people I trust for advice and tips on how to improve. I take workshops, webinars, and read books to become a better version of myself. And I make sure to keep the Lord as the center of my life. I pray everyday, and I always ask for wisdom to make better decisions in life.

I hope that you will also be able to love yourself first, as this will be the foundation for moving forward and passing that love on to those around you!

I Moved on From Rejection

I have experienced being rejected many times in my life. I have learned to stop taking them personally, and it has been liberating to get over them in time. However, some rejections were just more painful than usual. These usually involved people whom I really liked, and they did not feel the same way towards me. They made me question whether I was good enough for them, and whether I am capable of being loved at all. After working on myself, I have learned that I am enough, and that I am worthy of being loved. It is simply a matter of knowing that I cannot please everyone, and that is okay.

Being rejected by people that I liked was tough because I have already invested so much in them. I felt for them, and I visualized a future with them. In order to separate myself from the idea of them, I visualized a future by myself. I imagined achieving my dreams and goals out of my own efforts. I also worked on myself by maximizing the present. I stopped myself whenever I yearned to be with them, and whenever I felt like I was better off with them. I reminded myself that they have already said no to me. It is about time that I say yes to myself.

I tried to stay friends with those who have rejected me, but if it was too unhealthy to stay in touch with them, then I blocked them out of my life. I chose to communicate with those who truly had my back. I read books on self-empowerment. I did not find fulfillment in other people. Instead, I solely focused on self-care and accepting myself for who I really am.

I joined workshops and networking opportunities in order to meet new people. It was an effective wake-up call to expose myself to more people, as this reminded me of the fact that there are truly plenty of people out there who can be potential friends and contacts. It is totally unnecessary to limit myself to those who would rather stay away from me.

I have also rejected people in the past, and this was usually because we did not share the same values and interests. I chose people who shared similar interests and values because this was more sustainable in the long run. I can say now that I have made the right choice, and I am writing books in order to help people know themselves better and make smarter choices in life. I hope that my books will also help others decide which people are the best ones for them, and how they can move forward from being rejected by those whom they liked.

I hope that being rejected will redirect you back to yourself. You deserve to treat yourself well instead of pleasing those who do not even want to be with you. Rejections are simply redirections. It is up to you to accept them as a way to begin again, because life is too short to dwell on those who do not even accept us for who we are.

I Developed My Skills

Being on my own has enabled me to rely on myself for self-improvement. I realized that I finally had the time to pursue my interests. I started with knitting, then I moved on to crochet. When I was able to use my crochet skills for charity work during the pandemic, I knew that I had it in me to commit to a daily project. So, I gave journaling a try by enrolling in a journaling webinar.

I have always been a writer, so journaling became natural to me. It became my daily routine. I wrote about my feelings, my plans, and my dreams. In no time, I was writing the outline and draft for my manuscript. This would later become my first book, *Speak Blog Live*, which was published in October 2021.

By developing my writing, I was able to flesh out the ideas for my first book. By writing my first book, I was able to fulfill my lifelong dream of becoming a published author. And by writing everyday, I was able to write more books. This happens to be my fourteenth published book. I am happy that I took a leap of faith when I enrolled in that journaling class. I still journal everyday, and it gives me the writing practice and creative outlet that I constantly need.

I am grateful for the drive and determination to develop my skills. It is self-love in action, because it was essential for me to believe in myself in the first place. I wanted to improve as a person, and I needed to create things which were truly my own. I knew that it was important to apply my skills in order to have quality output. I also understood that I had to be humble enough to become a beginner. By being a self-starter, I was able to push myself to begin again and create. By being hungry for change and self-improvement, I was able to acquire and develop creative skills. And by committing to my creative process, I was able to change my life and have a thriving writing career which I have started from scratch.

I want you to know that it is okay to be awful at the beginning of everything. Learning means that you will get better in time. I want you to know that humility is the product of being aware of your limitations. I want you to know that progress naturally occurs when you want it to happen, and when your efforts bear fruit. I want you to know that creativity is not an overnight process. Creativity is all about hard work and the story that you want to tell. It is up to you to do the work while sharing your story. It is all up to you.

You can make incredible things happen when you develop your skills and live a creative life. It is all about working hard and using your creativity to show the world that you are making a difference!

I Built My Confidence

There was a time when my confidence was tied to how well I did in school, and later, at work. While I always did my best and became a top performer in my field, I realized that equating my confidence with how well I excelled on the job was not sustainable in the long run. I have proven this to be true when I left the corporate world in order to become a full-time freelancer a few years ago. I kept a steady stream of clients, and I did my job well. But I knew that I needed to work on myself in order to be confident in myself, just because I was sure of myself and my skills.

The pandemic has given me the extra time that I needed to work on myself. I read books which helped me identify the issues I needed to work on, such as self-esteem and self-acceptance. I learned how to accept myself by journaling and acknowledging that my flaws are part of who I am. I also learned that I needed to work through my past traumas. I guided myself through several journaling prompts and also, by working on each experience in detail.

I am not a psychologist, nor am I an expert in the field of mental health. I am only sharing what worked for me. I knew that I was capable of healing myself, so I used all the time I had at home during the pandemic to overcome my own personal issues such as grief. I learned that grief is a lifelong process, and it is up to me to deal with it as it comes in waves. I learned that confidence was a result of being sure of myself and my abilities, so I developed my skills. And when I was finally able to process my emotions and experiences, I wrote my books so that I can share what worked for me and enabled them to help other people better themselves.

I can now say that I am confident in myself and my abilities. I am aware that I am a work in progress. There will always be days when I need to work on myself a little more, and that is fine. It is up to me to be self-aware and to guide myself into doing what is best for me. It is also important to know that I have the right people to help me as I write books that help others with their own struggles.

If you are lacking in self-confidence, I suggest that you take up journaling. Write down the things that make you insecure, and list down the ways that will help you overcome them. I know that there is no right or wrong way to go about this. Use your own skills and experiences to improve yourself and to uplift yourself. You have plenty of time to better yourself, so start building your confidence today! It is all about knowing yourself and being aware that you are capable of changing your life for the better.

Lastly, always remember that you love yourself. You are capable of making things happen because you are worthy of good things! I have complete trust and faith in you.

I Learned to Thrive Alone

Being alone is a necessary survival skill. I believe that we all need to learn how to befriend ourselves and be comfortable in our own company. This has led me to write my book *I Befriended Myself*. I wanted to help people become their own best friend. It is not easy, but with a little work and consistent efforts, it can be done. It is also doable once you already know yourself. Let me share with you the systems that worked for me in order to thrive alone.

Like any friendship, it begins with an introduction. I re-introduced myself to myself. I shared my interests and passions with myself. I shared my favorite movies, books, music, and art. I worked out and shared my fitness journey with myself. And I prayed for myself, because there were times when I was drowned with the intentions of my loved ones.

It may seem strange to share your own life with yourself, but that is the whole point. We are not used to the idea of living for ourselves, so we find being acquainted with ourselves weird. But being aware of who we really are is necessary to the process of thriving alone. Once we know ourselves well, it will be easier for us to spend time alone and even enjoy our own company.

The next step is to have room for growth. Learn new skills. Enjoy a new hobby. Read books. Travel. Eat at restaurants alone. Have coffee alone. You will grow as a person as you spend more time by yourself. You will also be able to appreciate your own company, and this will lead to self-love and self acceptance. You will also realize how easy it is to thrive alone, once you are capable of making yourself happy by giving yourself what you want and need in this life.

Finally, you need to understand that you are all that you have got. Sure, you have your loved ones, and the life that you have built for yourself. But you need to realize that you will be by yourself more often than not. At the end of the day, you will be with yourself, whether you have someone beside you or not. So, always honor yourself because it is the only self that you have got. Always begin and end the day with an appreciation for yourself. Always have the mindset of growth, possibilities, and improvement. And always be determined to work on yourself so that you can constantly improve.

And once you are able to thrive alone, you will realize that life is an amazing journey that is full of opportunities for self-discovery and self-growth. Take yourself to the next level by learning the art of thriving alone. It will transform you into an independent individual who is capable of being happy, no matter what. Remember, life is too short to take yourself and your life for granted.

You will definitely love forward when you know how to thrive alone.

I Dated to Marry

The secret to finding the love that you deserve is to first realize that you are worthy of that love. You are worth loving because you love yourself first. You are worth the attention, the care, and the time because you know that you would not settle for anything less. And once you realize that the love you deserve is the unselfish kind, then you will realize that dating to marry is the only way to go.

I am aware that there are people who do not wish to get married, and there are also those who prefer to be single all their lives. That is fine. I am writing this chapter because I myself date to marry, and I do intend to settle down at some point. I am here because I have been through toxic relationships which made me feel like I did not deserve the kind of love that is worth fighting for. My former partners only cared about themselves. They were ashamed of me because we did not belong to the same background, and they refused to support my writing career. I have had enough of these people who were too self-centered to love and support me completely. It was heartbreaking to leave them behind, but I had to do that for my own sake.

Once I was free from these selfish people, I took some time to journal and really get to know myself. I solved my own issues and gave myself solutions such as books, webinars, and workouts. I spent time writing my books and letting go of things I no longer needed. I also addressed my own insecurities, and I reminded myself that it is okay to be imperfect. No one has it all figured out. It was when I realized that it is okay to be myself that I was finally able to attract quality people. Then, I found my current partner, who supports and accepts me for who I really am.

It was when I found the right person for me that I realized that I am dating someone whom I intend to marry in the future.

I know that I deserve this love because I worked on myself and on my capacity to love. My partner has also worked on himself, and he continues to do so. We strive to become a work in progress, and together, we make the journey more meaningful and bearable. I know that someday, I will spend the rest of my life with him. For now, I am spending my life loving and caring for myself.

Date to marry, yet learn to be merry on your own. You have all the time to improve yourself and change your life for the better. You have everything that you need to build a life that you can be proud of and find the answers to life's questions. Your journey does not end in self-love, because you can potentially share this with another person. Remember, it is all about balance.

I Dated Intentionally

Dating intentionally stems from knowing what I truly deserve. After journaling and getting to know myself better, I realized that I wanted to be in a relationship with someone who was willing to commit to me. I knew that I was ready to be in a long-term relationship, and I wanted to be with someone who was sure of me. It was time to finally date like a grown-up.

I was dating people who were still getting to know themselves, and were exploring the dating scene. I have gone through that in my 20s and early 30s, and it was fun but unsustainable. It was also sad because the people I met were not ready to settle down, or even date one person at a time. I found this shallow and lonely. I knew that I had to leave this scene, so I left my last relationship with someone who was not only unsupportive of me and my writing career, but also unwilling to marry me someday.

I started by taking a break to read, write my books, and eat out alone. Being my own best friend helped me move forward without going back to aimless dating. I was done with people who were not happy with commitment and growing old together. I wanted to be in a loving relationship, not just a partnership with someone who did not see me in his future.

Because I love myself, I wanted to be with someone who also sees my worth and gives me what I deserve. Luckily, I found my current partner who is passionate about his own interests and sees me as an equal. He respects me and he appreciates my work. Most of all, he encourages me to do my own thing and to pursue my passions. I love that he keeps himself happy with his own hobbies, and he loves his family. I see a future with him, and I am happy that he values commitment and family life. I think I found someone who is here for the long haul.

I know that dating intentionally can be overwhelming at the beginning, but trust me, it can be done. Start by knowing what you want, and looking for who you really want to be with. Do not settle. Be choosy, and get to know people very well. Ask help from your friends and family. Look for qualities in the people that you meet that are important to you. Have some non-negotiable terms such as commitment and being God-fearing. Never compromise. Always know what you want, and stick to it. Never give up on yourself.

Do not be afraid of losing your chances of dating people because you are intentional. Trust me, once you meet the right person for you, you will be grateful that you changed your perspective in dating and relationships. You deserve a better relationship, and you need this because you love yourself.

Once you love and date intentionally, you will have the best days of your life ahead of you!

I Learned to Say No

I realized that I said yes more than I should in the past. There were times when I was obliged to do things, so I proceeded with caution. These things usually ended badly in the end, so I made it a priority to recover from these incidents and learn from them. There were also people who were simply toxic and were very demanding from the beginning. I decided to say no to them once and for all, and I simply walked away from them.

Being free from people who did not have the best intentions was an act of self-love. I knew that I was better off without them, and I was right. My life instantly improved after leaving them. It was difficult at first because I was dependent on them for praise and approval, so I had to train myself to know that these people were fake and selfish. They were also backstabbers, and I discovered that they were spreading rumors about me. So, I learned how to depend on myself for praise and approval moving forward, and it has been helping me produce more engaging work since then.

Saying no also meant that I looked for new interests and hobbies. I learned how to knit and crochet, which then introduced me to a new set of friends. I also learned how to write books, which introduced me to my readers and friends who turned into readers.

The key is to stay authentic and true to yourself as you navigate through these new interests and activities. Be more discerning, and learn to pick better friends this time. As for the materials that you will use in these hobbies, invest in yourself by choosing high quality tools and materials. You deserve to have the best time with your new interests, and having the right equipment to excel in your chosen hobbies will make you feel good about yourself.

When you say no to people and experiences that make you feel small, you are giving yourself the chance to grow and finally feel better about yourself. You know that being with the wrong people will make you feel like you are not living a good life. You deserve to be happy, and the only way to do that is by giving yourself the chance and space to simply be yourself.

You have to start by saying yes to yourself. Say yes to the opportunities that excite you. Say yes to experiences that will teach you more about yourself and will help you grow. Say yes to people who genuinely care about you and who want to see you succeed. Say yes to a version of yourself that is the main character of your own story. Say yes to a bigger and better life.

At the end of the day, you should love yourself enough to know that you put yourself first. So, say no to being just a bit player in your own story. Be your own hero, and say no to being unhappy and unsatisfied in this life. Life is too short to be miserable, so save yourself now. Say yes to the opportunities that come your way and inspire you to become the best version of yourself.

I Journaled About Love

I started journaling during the pandemic because I wanted to express my feelings during this significant part of my life. I felt that this was a season of change since I was living and staying at home, which meant that I finally had the time to get to know myself better. It was difficult for me to have quiet moments before because I was always on the go. But when the lockdown happened, all I had was myself. So, I took advantage of the situation, and joined a journaling webinar.

I enjoyed the webinar so much that I started journaling immediately after the class. I surprised myself when I began journaling everyday, and before I knew it, I was already writing the outline and chapters for my first book. My book, *Speak Blog Live*, was eventually published in October 2021. It was a product of my daily journaling, and a symbol of my resilience during a challenging time.

Once I was able to write my books and develop my discipline and habit of writing everyday, I began to journal about love. I realized that if I wanted to have the love that I deserved, I needed to write about it. I started by listing down the qualities that I was looking for in a partner. Next, I wrote down how I could improve myself in order to become a quality partner. Then, I included sections about love in my daily journal entries, so that the concept of love will be something that was natural to me. It was important for me to get used to the idea of love in my life, so I continued to write about it.

Learning to love myself is a lifelong process. I must admit that there is still a long way to go for me. Journaling has helped me streamline the process of self-love by identifying my positive and negative qualities. For example, my love for writing has led me to become a published author. My discipline has brought me to where I am today, but I must admit that I can also become a workaholic. So, I worked on balancing my schedule so that I had enough time to pursue my passions. Exploring and enjoying my interests are important in inspiring me, and this will help me write better. Another example was my bravery when it comes to love, yet I also fell for the wrong people in the past. After working on myself by letting myself know that I deserve to be loved by a supportive and understanding partner, I finally found my current one. He supports me and he gives me the time and space to grow and shine. I really appreciate the work that I have done for myself.

Journaling has helped me realize that balance is important when it comes to self-love. When I finally learned how to love myself, I pushed myself to improve, and I started small. These small ways of self-improvement eventually made a difference in my life. Now, I am getting the love that I deserve, and it all began with self-love.

I hope that journaling will also allow you to know yourself better, so that you can share that love with others. You deserve the love that is worth writing about. You deserve the love that is patient and true.

So, write about it today!

I Became Happy No Matter What

I used to think that happiness was like being in a zone. It was a phase or dimension that I could be in for a limited time. However, as I got older, I realized that this was not true. Rather, I discovered that happiness was a choice. It was an everyday decision more than a disposition. After realizing that it was up to me to be happy, it became easier to find joy in everyday moments.

Happiness was not always easy to choose. There were moments in my life that really challenged me. When I lost some of my loved ones, I had to deal with grief. It was another healing process which made me choose happiness in order to move forward. When the pandemic happened, I learned to be happy even while I was at home all day long. I learned how to be productive and how to find joy in the simplest of things. I needed to diversify my career, so I became a published author while on lockdown. These experiences have shaped my character and defined my personhood. I became a better individual thanks to these experiences, and I became happier when I learned to survive and overcome them.

Once I was able to work on myself, I was able to choose happiness no matter what. This went hand in hand with finding self-love, which was one of the best gifts that I gave myself in my 30s. You too can achieve this kind of contentment and happiness earlier, or no matter what stage you are in life. Always know that since happiness is a choice, it is up to you to make it happen. Do it at your own pace, and do it for yourself.

One of the things that helped me stay happy everyday was to establish a routine. I worked out every morning because it made me feel good about myself. I enjoyed a healthy breakfast because I knew that I needed to be full and caffeinated in order to work effectively. I also had a system in place when it comes to work, which has helped me accomplish my tasks more efficiently. These parts of my day have helped me streamline my schedule and live a better life. I would not have it any other way.

The hardest part of choosing happiness is the beginning. I encourage you to journal in order to know yourself better. It is only through writing that you will learn how to start being happy each day. Do something that makes you happy everyday, and stick to that. Write down how you feel about it, and continue this until it becomes a habit. Before you know it, you are already choosing happiness.

It may be a struggle at first, but trust me, choosing happiness is one of the best decisions you can make. Do not be afraid to give yourself a chance to be happy. Remember, you only have one life to live. Make each day count.

Choose to be happy no matter what.

I Became Supportive of My Partner

I was able to support my own well-being by constantly working on myself. I started getting to know myself better through daily journaling. This habit has helped me establish boundaries. I was able to streamline my schedule by only focusing on the things that mattered to me. I had more peace of mind by staying away from toxic people. I stopped buying unnecessary objects, and I stopped distracting myself with mindless activities. I changed my life in a matter of months, and I can say that I am still a work in progress.

Once I was able to improve my life and leave my unsupportive partner, I stayed single. I did this because I wanted to date intentionally. I only went out with people who had the potential to be my lifelong partner. I dated to marry rather than dating just for the sake of doing so. It was all worth it because I found my partner who was also dating to marry. We shared the same values, and we had similar dreams. It was easy to be in a relationship with someone who I can truly say is my partner in life.

I supported his own dreams because I knew that he had a vision in life, and he made me feel part of it. I did not feel excluded from his dreams, and he shared how he wanted me to be in his life for a long time. I was happy to finally be with someone who knew what he wanted, and who knew how to get there. It was easy to support him, and it became an act of self-love for me as well.

I knew that I deserved a partner who treated me well and had a lot of dreams in life. He was hardworking, but he still made time for his family and me. He took care of his cats, and he still had time for himself. He lived a balanced life and he did not compromise his values to live well.

I hope that you will find a partner who can be your companion for life. You deserve someone who has solid values, dreams, and habits. I know that it is easier to settle for someone who seems interested in you but does not have dreams and goals. But you need to understand that life is not about what you are enjoying right now. It is about thinking long-term and seeing yourself with someone who can make you happy and content for the rest of your life. You need to know yourself well before you can truly be with the right person, so work on yourself today. Then, list down what you want your partner to have. List down your non-negotiable values, and then write down where you can find a partner who meets your criteria.

Be a quality person, and trust me, it will not be difficult attracting the right partner when you have a good head on your shoulders and a kind heart.

I Left Toxic Relationships

Before I was able to leave toxic relationships, I worked on myself first. I made sure that I was aware of my strengths and weaknesses. I journaled everyday to know myself better, and I listened to feedback from the people around me. I made sure that I was working on my areas of weakness, and I developed my skills. I worked out everyday, and I read books to feed my mind. The pandemic has allowed me to spend more time on myself, and I took advantage of my extra time at home. Before I knew it, I was able to build an excellent relationship with myself, which centered around self-improvement, fitness, and writing.

When I became a published author, I quickly observed that not everyone was happy for me. There were some people who made fun of me and my work, and I realized that this was no longer about me. This was already on them. So, I left those people who could not find joy in my fulfillment. I left those who could not accept the fact that I worked hard to make my dreams come true. At first, it was scary to leave these people behind, since

I knew some of them all my life. But it took some time before I noticed that leaving them was worth it, because I was finally able to have a lighter heart and a happier soul.

I also left my partner who was unhappy with my achievements. He was unfulfilled in his own personal life, so it was not surprising that he could not be happy for me. It was heartbreaking to be with someone who found validation in putting his partner down, and it was about time that I ended things with him. Once I became single again, I worked on myself and kept myself going. I reminded myself of what I wanted in a partner, and my ex was not that to me. In the end, I found the right person for me after all the work I did on myself after my breakup. It was all worth it, because my current partner supports me and my work. He makes me feel happy even when I am just being myself.

Always remember that leaving toxic relationships is necessary in order to achieve personal growth. You need to rely on yourself and you have to be strong on your own. You may find someone who can be a worthy partner to you, but you need to be able to stand on your own first. You need to have a healthy relationship with yourself before you can love someone else to the fullest.

You will never be alone when you have yourself. So, leave those who cannot appreciate you for who you really are, and surround yourself with people who truly care about you. Life is too short to be with those who drag you down. You will notice that life will be so much better when you love yourself and you have the right people around you.

I Became the Partner that I Wanted to Have

Working on myself after leaving my unsupportive ex was difficult at first. I needed to pinpoint which of my characteristics were dragging me down. I identified them through journaling, and I researched new ways on overcoming them. I have been aware of them all my life, and I believe that I continue to be a work in progress. I just had to manage my weaknesses and build on my strengths.

For example, I knew that time management was not my greatest strength. So, I made my own planning system, which involved a paper planner and a pen. It worked for me, and I even wrote a book about it. *Speak Plan Live* is a book that I am very proud of because it is a testament to my determination to improve myself and share my learning with others. It became my reference book as well whenever I needed to remember how I planned and scheduled my tasks.

My self-improvement efforts have led me to become the partner that I wanted to have. I am aware that my previous relationships have ended because of my partners' lack of support and encouragement. So, I became a supportive partner to myself. I made sure that I was strong enough to push myself to fulfill my goals and duties. I also rewarded myself every time I became successful in attaining my goals. It was all about balance.

I ended up writing and publishing my books amidst my breakups and personal challenges. I met my current partner after being focused on being my own support system, and now, I can say that I am no longer needy and clingy. I am my own person, and my partner is simply there to guide me and to hold my hand as we both go through life.

To be the partner that you want to be, you need to work on your skills. Use your own strengths to fulfill yourself and realize your goals. Work on your areas of improvement. Give yourself time and space to heal and grow. Give yourself the chance to rise above your limitations and improve.

Being your own partner is only difficult at the beginning. You will need to consistently show up for yourself in order to become your own support system. You also need to be your best self in order to let yourself know that you can be better than you expect yourself to be. Life is too short to be mediocre and subpar.

Know that having a partner is optional. You can make it on your own. You will survive by yourself. This is why it is important to thrive without anyone else's help, and be capable of helping yourself. You will become a better person by being your own support system. And when you do meet a partner for life, you will become a better and more reliable partner.

Be the partner that you have always wanted for yourself, and you will realize that life has already given you the most valuable resource: yourself.

I Built a Life with My Partner

I made sure that I was already happy by myself before I even considered dating again. It was surreal to imagine that not very long ago, I was still pining for my former partner who did not even want what is best for me. When our relationship ended, I was able to focus on my own self. I made my own plans and dreams a reality, and before I knew it, I was certain that I was thriving alone. I was ready to consider dating again.

Unlike before, I no longer tried too hard when it came to dating. I knew what I wanted in a partner, and I was also aware of my strengths and weaknesses. I was conscious of my goal to date to marry. I was done with dating simply because I wanted to have fun. This mindset has enabled me to find a partner almost immediately, because I was very clear with what I wanted. And once I found him, we were able to build a life together.

This time, I was no longer alone. I knew that being with someone who supported me and my goals was a game changer. While we did enjoy each other's company and had a lot of fun together, we were also capable of supporting each other with our concrete plans and dreams. We were very transparent with who we really are, and we did not need to impress each other anymore. It was an easy, natural relationship which gave me more time and freedom to pursue my own goals as a published author. I was also encouraging him to go after his own dreams, which he is happily doing at the moment. I am happy with our healthy relationship dynamics.

In order to build a life with your partner, you must first know who you really are and what your purpose in life is. Next, you must be clear about your goals in a relationship, as well as what you look for in a lifelong partner. Consider your own values, and think of how far you are willing to compromise. Stick to your values, and listen to your own instincts. Be very particular about the kind of partner you desire, and the relationship that you yearn for. It is crucial to have the right partner in order to have an amazing life and peace of mind.

Do not be afraid to ask people questions. Ask for help if you want to be introduced to the right people. Try dating apps, join workshops in order to meet quality people, and be friendly. You need to put yourself out there without looking and being desperate. Just be yourself!

Finally, remember that building a life together with your partner is a team effort. Is your date capable of being with you in a relationship? Is he or she ready to commit? Is he or she willing to be a team with you? You need to know the answer to these questions before you commit to that person that you like. Otherwise, it is better for you to pursue someone else whose values align with yours.

It is all a matter of knowing what you want, and how much you love yourself that makes being in a relationship with the right person possible.

I Focused on My Relationship

I am fortunate to have another chance to be in a relationship. This time, the person I am with does not have red flags. I have known him for years, and I have watched him thrive in his career. I know that I am with him for the right reasons, and he is also with me because he really loves me. I now have time to focus on my relationship.

This has not always been the case for me. As I have shared in the previous chapters of this book, I used to be with people who refused to support me and my career. They were still finding their places in this world, and it was difficult for me to navigate through these unhealthy relationships. As a result, I had to focus on myself when these relationships ended. And when I was already secure with myself, I found myself growing as an individual when I was already with the right person.

Focusing on my relationship meant that I was being myself with the person who was also being himself. We did not have to change or compromise anything with us. Sure, every relationship has sacrifices, but ours were not major sacrifices and adjustments. I am happy that this is the case for us. It is an easy partnership because we are finally right for each other.

If you are looking for the right partner for you, I suggest that you become that partner yourself first. Find yourself before you look for that partner. And when you eventually become the person that you are truly meant to be, then you will find the right person for you.

Finally loving yourself is the key to loving forward. You need to love yourself first before becoming the ideal partner to someone else. Use the lessons that you learned to better yourself and to become the partner that you aspire to be. Do not be in a relationship just because you intend for it to end. Rather, work on your relationship as you continue to work on yourself.

May you find the love that you are looking for within you, and may it lead you to a lifetime of happiness and fulfillment!

About the Author

Samantha Gail B. Lucas

Samantha Gail B. Lucas has been blogging on her website, www.speakoutsam.com, since May 2017. She has since attended several conferences, workshops, and networking opportunities through her website. She regularly shares her favorite local finds, foodie adventures, charitable advocacies, and media partnerships. She graduated with an AB Humanities degree from the University of Asia and the Pacific. Finally Loving Forward is her fourteenth published book. She currently resides in Quezon City, Philippines.

www.ingramcontent.com/pod-product-compliance
Lightning Source LLC
LaVergne TN
LVHW041226080526
838199LV00083B/3399